This
Cup Full of Wishes
belongs to:

Tellwell Talent
www.tellwell.ca

ISBN
978-0-2288-0764-3 (Hardcover)
978-0-2288-0763-6 (Paperback)

To my loves Kailash, Kailan, Ved, Vikash and Shivani…

      . . . and to LOVE.

To feel what it's like

to have the heat of the sun in your heart,

the twinkle of the stars in your eyes,

and the glow of the moon

of what it feels like to come home.

A Cup Full of Wishes

NARISSA LILA SAWH

Quietly, while you were asleep one night . . .
The stars and I were talking.

I said to them that I was going to
catch all the shooting stars and
put them into a magical cup . . .

A magical cup full of wishes of all the sweetest things.

I wish you a cup full of laughter and smiles of delight as beautiful and warm as the morning sunlight.

I wish you so many playful puppies...

to wake you up with a face full of kisses
and wet-nosed tickles to your tummy.

I wish you music that fills your heart and moves your feet . . . to make them dance with every beat.

I wish you clouds so if you ever fall, you will land safely on a big fluffy cotton ball.

I wish you warm rain to enjoy jumping in puddles again and again.

I wish you many seashells so you can listen to the sound of the ocean

...and not even have to rub on suntan lotion.

I wish you a field full of colourful flowers, so you can chase butterflies and birds for hours upon hours.

I wish you moonlight to always light your way

...back to the sky where all the stars play.

And when you are tired and bedtime is night,

I wish you dreams full of rainbow slides

To sweep you back up and catch the sky.

And while you are asleep, all snuggly and warm, know that all my love will keep you safe from any storm.

I wish you all of this, and so much more,
because you are everything

. . . I could have ever hoped for.

CPSIA information can be obtained
at www.ICGtesting.com
Printed in the USA
LVHW072252301121
704929LV00005B/23